CANADA

Minnesota

Wisconsin

Michigan

Iowa

Nebraska

Illinois

Indiana

Ohio

New Hampshire

Vermont

Maine

New York

Massachusetts

Rhode Island

Connecticut

Pennsylvania

New Jersey

West
Virginia

Delaware

Maryland

Virginia

Washington,
D.C.

Kansas

Missouri

Kentucky

Oklahoma

Arkansas

Tennessee

North Carolina

South
Carolina

Mississippi

Alabama

Georgia

Texas

Louisiana

Florida

N

W

E

S

OHIO

WEST VIRGINIA

Newport

Big Bone Lick

Carter Caves

Licking River

Kentucky River

Frankfort

Lexington

Slade

INDIANA

Louisville

Fort Boonesborough

Natural Bridge

Ohio River

Fort Knox

Bardstown

Berea

Breaks Interstate Park

ILLINOIS

Owensboro

Hodgenville

Benham

VIRGINIA

Mississippi River

Mammoth Cave

Corbin

Green River

Cave City

Cumberland River

Cumberland Falls

Bowling Green

Lake Cumberland

Paducah

MISSOURI

Wickliffe Mounds

Hopkinsville

Kentucky Lake

Land Between the Lakes

Lake Barkley

TENNESSEE

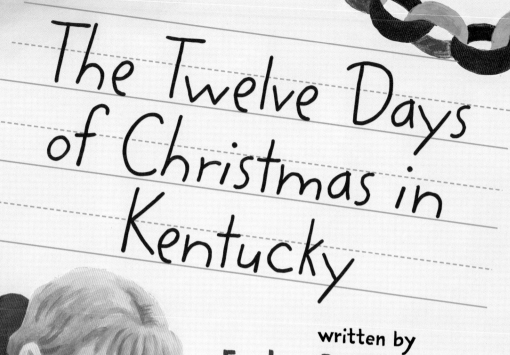

The Twelve Days of Christmas in Kentucky

written by
Evelyn B. Christensen

illustrated by
Kent Culotta

STERLING CHILDREN'S BOOKS
New York

Yipppppppppeeeeeeeeee, Martin!

Mom and Dad just told me you get to spend twelve days of the Christmas holidays with us. I'm SO excited! We're already busy planning fun places around Kentucky we can take you so you can get to know our wonderful state a bit. Kentucky is full of variety—we've got the **Appalachian Mountains**, beautiful horse farms in the Bluegrass Region (where we live, in **Lexington!**), tons of rivers and lakes, and even big caves.

Pack warm clothes because it's cold here in December. It might even snow, but we don't count on it. I'm also busy picking out fun gifts for you—one for each day of your visit. The one for the very last day includes tickets to a really special event, but it's a secret, so you'll have to wait to find out about it. When you come to Kentucky, get ready for some awesome music, yummy food, amazing crafts, big animals (and some small ones, too), and oodles of fun. I can't wait for you to get here!

Your cousin from Kentucky,

Marybeth

Dear Mom and Dad,

What a full day! Marybeth, Aunt Susan, and Uncle Stephen met me at the Louisville airport with cheers and high-fives. Right away, Marybeth gave me my first gift—a cardinal in a tulip poplar, the Kentucky state bird and tree. The tree will have yellowish-green flowers and may grow as tall as 150 feet! Marybeth said the cardinal's name is Daniel for Daniel Boone, Kentucky's most famous pioneer. I'm going to call him Danny. He's a real hoot.

Our first stop was the Louisville Zoo. Lots of awesome animals! My favorites were the naked mole rats. They're so ugly, they're cute. They live underground in groups, like ants, but the zoo had glass where we could see them in their tunnels. They have four big front teeth, and they can move the two lower ones sideways, like chopsticks. How cool is that?!

Next we went to the Louisville Slugger Museum and Factory, famous for its baseball bats. I got to hold a bat Mickey Mantle used, see bats being made, and take home my own mini-bat. Outside is a HUGE bat—68,000 pounds of steel, 6 stories tall!

Your exhausted but happy Kentucky traveler,
Martin

↖ us!

Dear Mom and Dad,

Today we went sailing down the Ohio River in a flatboat. Well, not really, but it was fun to pretend in the Thomas D. Clark Center for Kentucky History museum in Frankfort. We were pioneers, having to make tough decisions about what to take to Kentucky and what to leave behind, 'cause the boat didn't have much room. Danny made it clear we weren't allowed to leave <u>him</u>!

Frankfort is the capital city of Kentucky. After seeing tons of cool things at the museum, we went to the Capitol building. The inside is amazing! I can't imagine how all those marble columns and stairs were built. We saw a statue of Abe Lincoln. I knew he was one of America's greatest leaders and was president when we fought the Civil War that freed the slaves, but I didn't know he was born in Kentucky 'til Marybeth told me. Later we saw the statue of another great Kentucky-born leader, Whitney M. Young, Jr. He helped to work for equal rights for all people.

Outside the capitol was the largest Floral Clock in the US. In the summer it holds more than 10,000 flowers!

Your new history buff,
Martin

Dear Mom and Dad,

This morning, we went with a group of friends to the Kentucky Reptile Zoo in Slade. It has about 100 kinds of reptiles, including more than 1,000 snakes! The really cool thing was to watch the owner "milk" a snake to get venom. He milks more than 600 snakes each week. The venom is used all over the world to help make medicine. Poor Danny was so nervous—afraid he might be a snake's lunch.

He was much happier on our next adventure—hiking to the top of Natural Bridge. The view up there was awesome! The huge rock arch is a bridge that nature made all by itself.

In the afternoon, it was hooray for more animals! At the Newport Aquarium, we saw aquatic animals from around the world. One of the first we checked out was the Kentucky spotted bass, the state fish. Then we explored other exhibits. Marybeth's favorites were the jellyfish and the penguins. My favorites were the sharks. When we were in a glass tunnel, they were swimming over and around us, <u>really</u> close. And at Shark Central, we got to touch them! Surprise!—they felt rough like sandpaper.

Your future zoologist,
Martin

Natural Bridge

Dear Mom and Dad,

Today we visited a thoroughbred horse farm. Wow, those horses are sooo big! Marybeth told me Kentucky is famous for racehorses. Maybe one of the horses we saw will be a Kentucky Derby winner someday—that's <u>the</u> important horse race, held in Louisville each May.

Guess what! We got to groom a horse. We brushed its coat, combed its mane, and used a pick to clean its hooves. Danny helped with the mane. Did you know horses' hooves get trimmed, sort of like our fingernails? They also wear metal shoes that are supposed to be lucky. Marybeth gave me four! We played a game trying to toss the horseshoes around a stake. If I hang them on a wall, I have to remember to point them up—so the luck runs in, not out.

Tonight we saw four miles of gigantic Christmas light displays at the Kentucky Horse Park here in Lexington. At the end were rooms full of electric model trains, a petting zoo, and reindeer! I wonder if horses are jealous that Santa chooses reindeer to pull his sleigh instead of them.

Feeling lucky to be in Kentucky,
Martin

Dear Mom and Dad,

Guess where we went today! The place where the government stores most of our country's gold. Its official name is the U.S. Bullion Depository, but since it's at Fort Knox, that's what people usually call it. We couldn't go inside, though. <u>Absolutely</u> <u>NO</u> <u>visitors</u> are allowed!!! It's locked up tighter than tight with all kinds of security like alarms, land mines, electric fences, armed guards, and a vault door that weighs over 20 tons. It's a good thing the golden foil-covered chocolate bars Marybeth gave me were not golden bars from the Depository. Otherwise, we might be in big trouble.

On the way, we stopped at Federal Hill Mansion in Bardstown, all decorated for Christmas, 1800s-style. That's where Stephen Foster was inspired to write "My Old Kentucky Home," the state song. Danny entertained us by singing his own version of it.

We also stopped in Hodgenville, where Abe Lincoln was born. We walked up 56 steps that represent the 56 years he lived. At the top is a log cabin like Lincoln's birthplace. It reminded me that people can do great things even if their beginnings don't seem great.

Wondering if I'll do great things,
Martin

Something else golden in KY:

goldenrod, the state flower.

On the fifth day of Christmas,
my cousin gave to me . . .

5 golden bars

4 lucky shoes, 3 swift sharks, 2 great leaders,
and a cardinal in a tulip poplar.

Dear Mom and Dad,

We're visiting Aunt Susan's friend Meg in Paducah today, and we went to the National Quilt Museum, the biggest quilt museum in the world! We saw tons of amazing quilts. Marybeth's gift to me was six quilt squares, each a different pattern. My favorite is "Log Cabin," because the name reminds me of Lincoln. Marybeth is learning to quilt. She said she tried to make me a quilt square, but Danny kept pulling the threads out.

Quilting has been important in Kentucky since pioneer days. Recently, people have painted huge quilt squares on their barns. They're part of the Kentucky Quilt Trails. Marybeth and I are competing to see who can spot the most as we travel. So far, Danny is ahead of both of us!

Meg wanted to cook me some "real" Kentucky food. She gave me a choice of soup beans and cornbread, burgoo (a kind of stew), chicken 'n' dumplings, or Hot Browns. I picked Hot Browns—an open face sandwich with turkey, tomato, bacon, and cheese sauce. Super yummy! We also had blackberry cobbler since blackberries are Kentucky's official fruit.

Feeling full of scrumptious Kentucky food,
Martin

Yum!
Blackberries!

On the sixth day of Christmas,
my cousin gave to me . . .

6 handmade quilt squares

5 golden bars, 4 lucky shoes, 3 swift sharks, 2 great leaders,
and a cardinal in a tulip poplar.

Dear Mom and Dad,

Can you imagine a huge sinkhole, in the middle of the night, swallowing eight museum cars? Sounds like something out of a movie, doesn't it? But that actually happened at the National Corvette Museum, in Bowling Green. We heard about it when we visited there today. Getting to see sports cars put together by people and robots at the assembly plant was also pretty amazing.

Dinosaur World in Cave City was our next stop. Talk about a time warp—going from ultra-modern robots to prehistoric creatures. There were over 150 life-size dino models for us to see. We also got to do a fossil dig. Danny was extra good at that.

Marybeth said no dinosaur bones have been found in Kentucky, but mammoths and mastodons lived here. So we spent extra time with the mammoths. I would not have wanted to be an early human having to hunt one of those huge animals for food. Too scary! Uncle Stephen told me that mastodon bones found at Big Bone Lick in northern Kentucky in 1739 started the study of fossils in America.

Your budding paleontologist,
Martin

On the seventh day of Christmas, my cousin gave to me . . .

7 woolly mammoths

6 handmade quilt squares, 5 golden bars, 4 lucky shoes, 3 swift sharks, 2 great leaders, and a cardinal in a tulip poplar.

Dear Mom and Dad,

Do you know what the longest cave system in the <u>whole world</u> is? Mammoth Cave. It's called mammoth 'cause it's so HUGE! It has more than 400 miles of explored passages, and today we got to tour part of it.

We saw awesome, beautiful rock formations—curvy ones like bacon, hanging ones like curtains, stalactites (that hold <u>tight</u> to the ceiling), stalagmites (that <u>might</u> grow to reach the ceiling), and best of all, Frozen Niagara! It really did look like a frozen waterfall.

I thought we'd see bats, but we didn't. Instead, we saw hundreds of cave crickets. Fun! Danny tried pretending to be a bat by hanging upside down but decided that wasn't for him. Our guide told us a disease called white-nose syndrome is sadly killing millions of bats in eastern North America, including many in Mammoth Cave. Park rangers are trying to stop the spread of it.

Our guide also told us some Mammoth Cave history. Can you believe that Native Americans were in the cave 4,000 years ago? Items they used have been found there. Exciting!

Your future spelunker (that's someone who explores caves),
Martin

Frozen Niagara!

Dear Mom and Dad,

We got our snow today! Just enough to look like white frosting. It didn't stick to the roads—a good thing, since we were traveling to Cumberland Falls.

Have you ever heard of a moonbow? It's like a rainbow, except with moonlight instead of sunlight. Cumberland Falls is the only place in the western half of the world it can be seen. We didn't see one, because we weren't there at night with a full moon, but we did see a rainbow in the mists of the falls. Beautiful!

We also saw lots of gray squirrels, Kentucky's official wild game animal. Silly Danny flew around showing them where <u>he</u> thought they should dig for nuts. A whitetail deer poked her nose through the trees, and a hungry raccoon decided to come out in the daytime to look for food.

Speaking of food—next we went to Corbin where a famous person had his first restaurant in the 1930s, cooking his special chicken recipe. Guess who?! Yep, we got to visit where Colonel Harland Sanders started KFC (Kentucky Fried Chicken). And, of course, we ordered some chicken!

Licking my fingers in Kentucky,
Martin

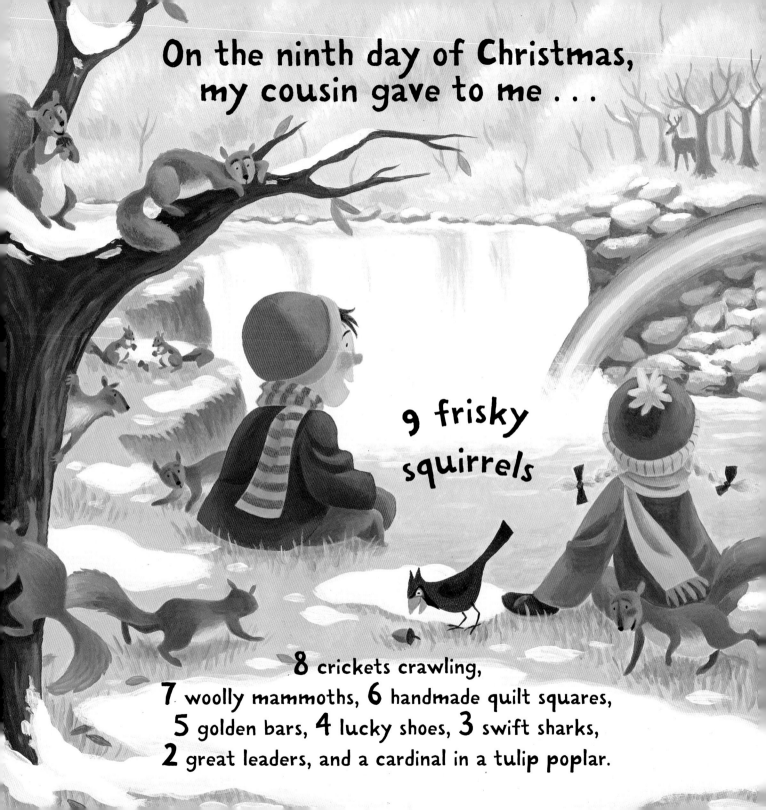

On the ninth day of Christmas,
my cousin gave to me . . .

9 frisky
squirrels

8 crickets crawling,
7 woolly mammoths, 6 handmade quilt squares,
5 golden bars, 4 lucky shoes, 3 swift sharks,
2 great leaders, and a cardinal in a tulip poplar.

Dear Mom and Dad,

I thought for sure Marybeth's gift today was a Christmas stocking joke—ten lumps of coal! She teased me about how bad I must've been this year, and Danny teased me by pulling my hair. But then Marybeth explained that coal is a big part of Kentucky's history.

At the Kentucky Coal Mining Museum in Benham, we learned what living in a coal camp was like for miners and their families. We even got to put on hardhats and go into a pretend mine. Coal has been both good and bad for Kentucky. Good because it brought jobs and money (people called it "black gold"), and because it provided inexpensive fuel for homes and factories. But bad because it was dangerous work for the miners and has caused problems for the environment.

One floor of the museum was about Loretta Lynn, a coal miner's daughter and famous country music singer. In the car, we listened to her music and also Bluegrass, Kentucky's state music. Those guitar and banjo pickers were great!

The proud new owner of some black gold,

Martin

On the tenth day of Christmas, my cousin gave to me . . .

10 lumps of black gold

9 frisky squirrels, 8 crickets crawling, 7 woolly mammoths,
6 handmade quilt squares, 5 golden bars, 4 lucky shoes, 3 swift sharks,
2 great leaders, and a cardinal in a tulip poplar.

Dear Mom and Dad,

Today, we stopped in Berea, the Folk Arts and Crafts Capital of Kentucky. Its shops were full of beautiful, handmade crafts. I hope y'all like the gifts I got y'all. (Does that sound Kentuckian? I'm practicing my y'alls.) Danny helped me choose them. Dad, I got you a pottery mug for your coffee. Mom, we watched a weaver finishing a set of placemats, so that's what I got you.

For more than 150 years, Berea College has encouraged Kentucky crafts (like weaving, pottery, and woodworking) and traditions (like folk dancing, storytelling, and music). We were lucky to get in on some music. A bunch of fiddlers and other musicians were jammin' and we clapped and sang along with them. One player even let me try a few strums on her dulcimer—that's the state musical instrument.

Next, we went to Fort Boonesborough, a replica of the fort founded by Daniel Boone (Danny's namesake!) in 1775. Marybeth said if I come back in the summer, I can see all kinds of demonstrations like spinning, candle dipping, soap making, and blacksmithing! Can I? Pleeease?

Hoping to come back,
Martin

On the eleventh day of Christmas, my cousin gave to me . . .

11 fiddlers fiddling

10 lumps of black gold, 9 frisky squirrels,
8 crickets crawling, 7 woolly mammoths,
6 handmade quilt squares, 5 golden bars, 4 lucky shoes,
3 swift sharks, 2 great leaders, and a cardinal in a tulip poplar.

Dear Mom and Dad,

I finally found out Marybeth's big secret: Tickets to the University of Kentucky Wildcats vs. University of Louisville Cardinals basketball game! Basketball in Kentucky is HUGE!!! And these are archrivals. Both have won national championships.

Marybeth has a basketball goal (they call it a goal, not a hoop, here in KY!) in her driveway, so to get warmed up for the big game we shot some baskets. Let me tell you— she's <u>good</u>! Kentucky kids must have basketball in their blood.

When we got to the game, Marybeth told me we had to cheer for both teams 'cause Aunt Susan went to U of L and Uncle Stephen went to UK. She handed me a red pompom and a blue one. Danny, however, made it clear he was only cheering for the Cardinals.

It was fun to watch the warm-ups with ball after ball whooshing through the baskets. The game was even more exciting. I won't tell you who won—I don't want the loser in this house to feel bad!

By the way, Marybeth says Kentucky has about fifty state parks and historic sites and I only saw four this trip. Want a suggestion for our summer vacation?

Missing Kentucky already,

Martin

On the twelfth day of Christmas, my cousin gave to me . . .

12 balls a-bouncing

11 fiddlers fiddling, 10 lumps of black gold, 9 frisky squirrels,
8 crickets crawling, 7 woolly mammoths,
6 handmade quilt squares, 5 golden bars, 4 lucky shoes,
3 swift sharks, 2 great leaders, and a cardinal in a tulip poplar.

Kentucky: The Bluegrass State

Capital: Frankfort • **State bird:** cardinal • **State flower:** goldenrod •
State tree: tulip poplar • **State butterfly:** viceroy • **State mineral:** coal •
State wild animal: gray squirrel • **State fruit:** blackberry • **State horse:** thoroughbred •
State fish: Kentucky spotted bass • **State fossil:** brachiopod • **State song:** "My Old Kentucky Home" • **State motto:** "United we stand, divided we fall"

Some Famous Kentuckians:

Muhammad Ali (1942–2016), born Cassius Clay, Jr. in Louisville, was an Olympic Gold Medalist in boxing, 3-time Heavyweight World Champion, and recipient of the Presidential Medal of Freedom. Considered one of the greatest athletes of the past century, he was also dedicated to working for peace and civil rights.

John James Audubon (1785–1851) moved to Kentucky at age 23. He was fascinated by nature and, as a painter, is especially famous for his 435 illustrations published as *Birds of America*.

Mary Breckinridge (1881–1965) came to Kentucky in 1925. She started, and for almost 40 years led, the Frontier Nursing Service, which provided medical care to poor, rural people.

Henry Clay (1777–1852) moved to Lexington when he was 20. A lawyer and skilled speaker, he served as both a U.S. senator and representative for Kentucky, as well as Secretary of State. He was called The Great Compromiser because he was good at helping opposing sides of an issue come to an agreement.

Jennifer Lawrence (1990–), an award-winning actress, was born and raised in Louisville. She is famous for her roles in *Silver Linings Playbook* and *The Hunger Games* series.

Bill Monroe (1911–1996), a mandolin player, songwriter, and singer, was born near Rosine. He is known as the Father of Bluegrass Music for developing a new style that combined Appalachian, blues, and gospel music. He named it after his band, the Blue Grass Boys. He received the National Medal of Arts award in 1995.

Garrett Morgan (1877–1963), born in Paris, Kentucky, was an African-American inventor. He created a smoke protection safety hood which firefighters used. He also invented the first three-position traffic signal.

Diane Sawyer (1945–), born in Glasgow, is an award-winning television news journalist and was 60 *Minutes'* first female reporter. She co-hosted *Primetime Live* and *Good Morning America* and hosted *ABC World News*.

To all my wonderful family, especially my terrific husband,
and to God, who loves us and gave us the best Christmas gift of all —E. B. C.

For Patrick —K. C.

STERLING CHILDREN'S BOOKS
New York

An Imprint of Sterling Publishing Co., Inc.
1166 Avenue of the Americas
New York, NY 10036

STERLING CHILDREN'S BOOKS and the distinctive Sterling Children's Books logo are trademarks of Sterling Publishing Co., Inc.

Text © 2016 by Evelyn B. Christensen
Illustrations © 2016 by Kent Culotta

ISBN 978-1-4549-1959-9

Distributed in Canada by Sterling Publishing
c/o Canadian Manda Group, 664 Annette Street
Toronto, Ontario, Canada M6S 2C8
Distributed in the United Kingdom by GMC Distribution Services
Castle Place, 166 High Street, Lewes, East Sussex, England BN7 1XU

For information about custom editions, special sales, and premium and corporate purchases, please contact Sterling Special Sales at
800-805-5489 or specialsales@sterlingpublishing.com.

Manufactured in China
Lot #:
2 4 6 8 10 9 7 5 3 1
07/16

www.sterlingpublishing.com

The original illustrations for this book were done in acrylic
on Strathmore 500 series, vellum-surfaced, bristol paper.
Designed by Andrea Miller and Paola Pagano